The Unready Rabbit

by Ruth Nivola
pictures by Claire Nivola

Chatto & Windus · London

First published in 1978 by Pantheon Books Inc., New York

First published in Great Britain in 1979 by
Chatto & Windus Ltd.
40 William IV Street
London WC2

For my grandson, *Alessandro,*
who was my inspiration and my first audience,
on his fourth birthday.

British Library Cataloguing in Publication Data

Nivola, Ruth
    The Unready Rabbit.
    I. Title II. Nivola, Claire
    823'.9'1J   PZ7.N/
    ISBN 0-7011-2407-5

Printed and bound in the U.S.A.

Once upon a time there was the sweetest little rabbit you could ever imagine. He had the fluffiest tail and great big eyes and he lived in a wonderful old house with his mother and father and sisters and brothers. He was a very good little rabbit too, very good indeed.

However, he did have one fault, and it grew worse and worse every day. He was a very untidy rabbit. When he got dressed in the morning, he would leave his pyjamas on the floor. When he came home from school he would drop his jacket on the staircase and his boots in the middle of the living-room. His hat often ended up in the bath. And once he even left his mittens on top of his peanut-butter sandwich. His brothers and sisters all had very tidy rabbit rooms — but the little rabbit's room looked like a pigsty.

One day everyone was going to a filmshow for a treat. His brothers and sisters were ready to leave in time to take a sleigh-ride down the hill to the cinema. The little rabbit, however, was not ready at all. First he could not find his shoes. He looked and looked all over the house and finally found them among the ashes in the fireplace. Then he could not find his hat. He looked and looked but it was nowhere to be found.

His mother and brothers and sisters were growing impatient. Finally everyone went off to the filmshow — except the little rabbit. And when they came back, having had a wonderful time, the little rabbit was still looking for his hat.

A few days later, everyone was going to a football match. There was a great hustle and bustle and the whole family was ready by the time Father Rabbit pulled up in the car and blew the horn — except for the little rabbit who was running round in circles. He had found his left shoe but not his right one and he had found his right mitten but not his left one.

Father Rabbit was very angry and drove away leaving the little rabbit behind. And when everyone came home with sweets and balloons, the little rabbit was still looking for his left mitten and his right shoe.

The day after that Grandpa Rabbit surprised his grandchildren with tickets for a puppet show. The little rabbit's brothers and sisters took their shoes off their shoe-racks, their jackets off the hooks, and their mittens and caps from the shelves, and they were ready in no time. But the little rabbit rushed around the house, first trying to find his boots, then his jacket and his mittens, and finally his cap. But when he found one thing he could not find the other, and when he found the other he had already lost the first one.

At last his grandpa, who was usually a patient man, lit his pipe, took his other grand-children by the hand, and left the little rabbit behind. And when they all came home still laughing about the puppet show the little rabbit was still looking for his mittens.

Not long afterwards Uncle Fireman-Rabbit came to visit the rabbit family. "Get ready," he announced, "and I'll take you all for a ride on a fire-engine." So everyone got dressed very fast (because they all knew that their Uncle Rabbit was a very busy fireman and did not have much time) and stood, ready at the door, as if they were going on parade. Only the little rabbit was missing. He was still rushing about trying to find this, and that, and the other thing.

So Uncle Fireman-Rabbit, in his very busy way, blew his whistle and everyone marched out of the door and off to the fire-station. The little rabbit was left behind again. And when everyone came back wearing big red firemen's helmets, the little rabbit was still looking for his jacket.

Soon after that the rabbits were invited to a birthday party. The little rabbit's brothers went to their cupboards and took out their best suits, and the little rabbit's sisters picked out their very best dresses. Only the little rabbit could not find his best suit. Then he spotted it under the kitchen sink. "This time," he thought, "I will be ready when everyone else is." He put on his suit very quickly, but found it was covered with dirt from the sink. When he saw how smart all his brothers and sisters looked, he felt ashamed to go with them.

So they all left for the party — except the little rabbit. And when everyone came home, each with a piece of birthday cake, the little rabbit was still trying to brush the spots off his suit.

One day the circus came to town. All the rabbits decided to go. No one took very long to get dressed — except the little rabbit.

Well, for the circus it was all right to be a little late, so everyone waited for him. While they were waiting they took out the money they had saved in their piggybanks to pay for the circus. Finally the little rabbit found his shoes, his mittens and his hat and was ready just like everyone else. All he needed was his piggybank. But, oh dear! Where was it?

Well, it was all right to be a little late for the circus, but not so late that you missed the clown. So everyone left in a hurry, while the little rabbit was still looking for his piggybank.

He had been sad to miss the filmshow and the football game. He had been sad to miss the puppet show, the ride on Uncle Rabbit's fire-engine, and the birthday party. But to miss the clown, that was too much for him. So he sat down in the big red rocking-chair and burst into tears. He cried and cried, and he was still crying when his friend the deer called. "Why are you crying on a sunny Sunday after-noon?" he asked.

"I could not find my piggybank so I could not pay for the circus and I missed the clown. My very, very favourite clown!" sobbed the little rabbit.

"Oh, well," replied the deer, "let's go and find your piggybank. Who knows? It might be in your room."

So the little rabbit and the deer went up–stairs together and when they opened the door of the little rabbit's room they were buried under all the belongings that came tumbling out.

"Well!" exclaimed the deer. "Now I know why you were always left behind. You are the untidiest little rabbit I have ever seen. How can you expect to find anything at all? Come on, let's clear up your room!"

So together they dug through the little rabbit's belongings and sorted them into piles. The toys went into the toy box, the books on the bookshelf, the shoes on the shoe-rack, the suits in the cupboard, all the socks into the top drawer. Sweaters went into the special drawer for sweaters and underwear into the bottom drawer.

They worked the whole day, until the room was a really neat rabbit room. When they picked up the last shirt from the floor, they found the piggybank underneath.

"Oh," the rabbit said, "if only I could still go to the circus!"

"It will be back soon," promised the deer. "And you will be able to go too —*if* you learn to keep your things where they belong."

The circus did come to town again soon, and this time the deer invited his little friend the rabbit and all his brothers and sisters to see it.

Well, believe it or not, the little rabbit was ready before anyone else, with his piggybank under his arm. He had found his jacket on the hook, his shoes on the shoe-rack, his mittens, his hat and even his scarf, on their shelves, and his piggybank standing neatly on the chest-of-drawers.

It had all been so simple and easy this time. The little rabbit got to the circus in time to sit in the very front row, from where he could see the clown nearby, and do you know what? When the clown pulled a stream of coloured handkerchiefs out of his ear and threw them into the air, the little rabbit caught them and handed them back all neatly folded. Then the clown waved to him and threw him a rose.

The end